The Dragon Meets a MERMAID

CHRISTINE DUBOIS

Tellwell Talent
www.tellwell.ca

ISBN
978-0-2288-5629-0 (Hardcover)
978-0-2288-5628-3 (Paperback)

Thank you!

To each one of you who has purchased this book, thank you so much for the support while I attend my Bachelor of Science in Nursing studies. I wrote this book to fundraise for my tuition.

Also, I would like to dedicate this book to my son, Tristan, who loves dragons, reptiles and fishing. We've spent lots of time together painting the illustrations you'll see in this book. It was a fun project that has given me time to spend with my son.

Warm regards,
Christine Dubois

If you scan this image with your phone (open the camera like you are going to take a picture), it will take you to my Facebook page so you can like and follow!

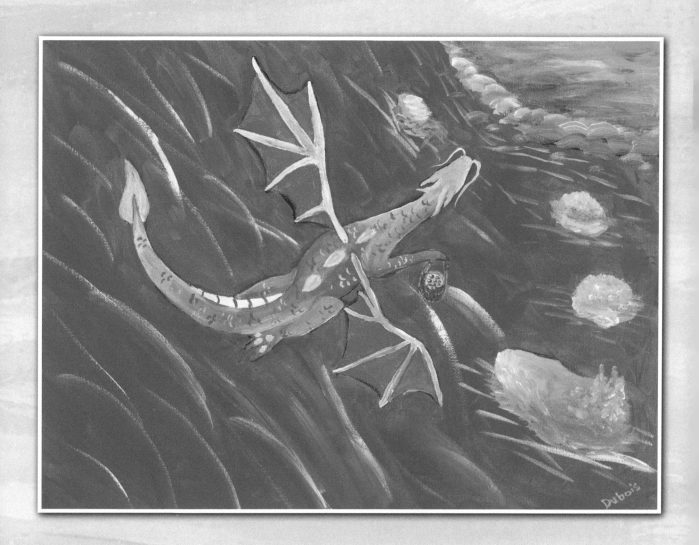

Levi was a dragon. He enjoyed flying to different islands to pick berries. Levi had great big wings that cast huge shadows on the villages below.

And he had a sneezing problem.

He started fires every time he sneezed, and the villagers were tired of it. Levi couldn't understand why the villagers didn't like him.

As Levi was passing over the village, a gust of wind flew up his nose and tickled his nose hairs. Levi let out a big sneeze.

"Abliberachoo!"

Levi accidentally started a fire. Again. It wasn't his fault though! He couldn't help it. Levi was terribly allergic to dust.

Levi was sad because no one liked him. He barely ever left his cave at the top of Wawatay Mountain. He didn't have anyone to share the beautiful view with. Levi cried all alone.

"Boo-hoo-hoo."

One day, Levi was picking berries when an old man named Otis startled him. Levi let out a great sneeze.

"Abliberachoo!"

This time, he lit the berry bush on fire.

Otis could see that Levi was troubled.

"What's wrong?" he asked.

"I am sad because people don't like me, and I can't stop sneezing," Levi wailed. "I don't mean to start fires. I just wanted to pick berries for everyone! A...A...Abliberachoo!"

"I know how to help you," said Otis, "but you
will have to make me a promise."

"I want an aquamarine gem," old Otis said.
"But the only way to get it is from the tears of a mermaid."

"This seems like a very strange request," Levi stammered through his tears,
"but if it means you can help me with the sneezing then I suppose I could
find some poor mermaid and make her cry. But is there any other way?"

"This is the only way. Now off you go, Levi!"

Levi, shaking his head, left for the quest.

Levi set out in search of a mermaid. He began looking
at each island nearby. He flew 'round and 'round but no
mermaids were to be found. Then he checked the beaches;
still no mermaids. Levi had to look farther away. He kept
searching way, way, way far out into the ocean as he flew
above the clouds. Levi was not going to give up! He checked
every wave very carefully. At the end of the Earth where the
moon meets the horizon, Levi finally found a mermaid!

When he found her, she was so kind and beautiful. Levi was smitten.

"Abliberachoo!" He blushed as he sneezed.

"Bless you," said the mermaid.

"Are you a real mermaid?" Levi asked in awe.

She chuckled. "Yes. 1 am as real a mermaid as you are a dragon. My name is Eve. What's your name?"

"My name is Levi. 1 have been looking for a mermaid for days! Old man Otis told me he would help me with my sneezing problem if 1 can find a mermaid and make her cry. Otis said 1 need to bring him back some aquamarine gems."

Eve smiled and said to Levi, "1 can help you with that!"

Levi remembered his promise to the old man. He had to make the mermaid cry! Just as he was about make her cry, he hesitated. No sneezes, no fire, not even a puff would come out of his mouth or nose. He was unable to make the mermaid cry because he was too kind.

Eve saw the kindness in Levi's heart, so she kissed him! Eve's kiss took Levi's breath away. Her kiss was like medicine, and his allergies were cured.

Levi, empty-handed but cured of his allergies, returned to face Otis.

"I failed to retrieve the aquamarine gem," Levi said. He was worried Otis would be upset. "The mermaid is far too lovely, so there is no way I would want to make her cry. I only want her to be happy."

"Sir, why do you need aquamarine?" Eve asked Otis.

"Oh, I don't need any aquamarine," Otis said. "I just wanted the dragon to stop burning the village down. Frankly, I didn't think mermaids were real. I thought Levi would be searching the ocean for at least a few weeks and leave us in peace!"

Eve began to cry after hearing how cruel the old man was. She cried many tears of aquamarine, but she refused to give any gems to cruel Otis! Instead, Eve and Levi decorated Levi's cave with the beautiful gems.

Levi no longer cared what the villagers thought of him. Instead, he spent time with lovely Eve, who enjoyed his company.

THE END

CPSIA information can be obtained
at www.ICGtesting.com
Printed in the USA
LVHW070320110721
692394LV00001B/5